Sophie and the Sidewalk Man

Stephanie S. Tolan

Illustrated by Susan Avishai

Four Winds Press ⚡ New York

Maxwell Macmillan Canada   Toronto
Maxwell Macmillan International
New York   Oxford   Singapore   Sydney

Four Winds Press
Macmillan Publishing Company
866 Third Avenue
New York, NY 10022

Maxwell Macmillan Canada, Inc.
1200 Eglinton Avenue East
Suite 200
Don Mills, Ontario M3C 3N1

Macmillan Publishing Company is part of
the Maxwell Communication Group of Companies.

First edition
Printed and bound in the United States of America

10 9 8 7 6 5 4 3 2 1

The text of this book is set in 13 point Sabon.
The illustrations are rendered in pencil.
Book design by Christy Hale

Library of Congress Cataloging-in-Publication Data
Tolan, Stephanie S.
Sophie and the sidewalk man / Stephanie S. Tolan. — 1st ed.
p.   cm.
Summary: Sophie is torn between her desire to buy a beautiful toy
hedgehog and her compassion for a hungry street person.
ISBN 0-02-789365-0
[1. Homeless persons—Fiction.] I. Title.
PZ7.T5735So 1992
[Fic]—dc20 91-17317

to the sidewalk people—
and those who care

I

Sophie stamped her feet to keep them warm. A cold wind was skittering dried leaves along the curb. People hurried by with their heads down and their hands in their pockets. Sophie looked up at the window where her friend Allison had waved a minute ago.

She jingled her lunch money in her coat pocket. If Allison didn't come out soon, there wouldn't be time to talk to Weldon. Sophie needed to talk to him this morning. She had something important to tell him.

Just then Allison came out the door and ran down the steps of the brick town house. "Come on, Soph," she called. "We don't have much time."

"What took you so long?" Sophie asked, hurrying to keep up with Allison's long strides. Allison was taller than Sophie, even though they were both eight.

"Sam hid my spelling book again," Allison said. "He's the worst brother in the whole world."

Sophie nodded. Allison was always complaining about Sam. Sophie was used to it.

"I didn't spend a single penny all weekend," Sophie told Allison. "I saved my whole allowance. I'm over halfway there! Weldon will be so excited."

"Maybe you'll be able to buy him before Christmas," Allison said. "Then you could put a stocking up, just for him. We do that every year for Tiger."

The two girls made their way between the hurrying grown-ups on the sidewalk. They passed the cleaners, the flower shop, and Rudowski's Market and stopped at the Humpty Dumpty Toy Store.

This morning Weldon, the hedgehog, was not in his usual place at the back of the window next to the unicorn. He was in the front, his pointed nose almost touching the glass. His bright black eyes looked right at Sophie.

"Good news!" Sophie told Weldon. "I have twenty-one dollars and seventy-eight cents saved up now. That's more than half. Only twenty dollars and twenty-one cents to go. Then you'll be able to come home with me!"

Sophie had been saving her money to buy Weldon since the end of September. That's when he had first appeared in the window. She had asked her mother to buy him for her, but her mother had said no. Weldon was too expensive.

Weldon *was* expensive. But that was because he was special. Mr. Berger, who owned the toy store, said he was imported from England. And he was handmade. There was a tag on the plaid bow around his neck that told the name of the person who had made him: Cecily Bottely. Mr. Berger called Weldon "a collector's item—one of a kind." That meant there was no hedgehog just like him in the whole world.

Pretty soon Weldon would belong to Sophie. Then she wouldn't have to talk to him through a window anymore. Mr. Berger had let her hold him

once, and she remembered just what he had felt like. His sharp prickles weren't as sharp as they looked. They were soft and tickly. His ears were made of shiny, smooth satin. Sophie touched the window. "Soon," she said. "I'll take you home with me soon."

Allison blew on her fingers to warm them. "He's a lot easier to see up here in the front."

Sophie grinned and nodded. Then the skin on the back of her neck prickled. He was easier for other people to see, too. "Why do you suppose Mr. Berger moved him?" she asked.

Allison shrugged. "So people will notice him."

"I don't *want* people to notice him," Sophie said. Then she had a terrible thought. "What if someone has been looking at him and that's why he's moved? What if Mr. Berger let someone else hold him?" Sophie swallowed hard. "What if someone else wants to buy him?"

Weldon was the very best animal in the window. He was even better than the gorilla with the leather face. Anyone could see that. And though he was very expensive, so was everything else in the store. Probably any grown-up who shopped there could afford to pay for him. It wouldn't take a grown-up months to save up the money. Christmas was coming. People bought lots of toys at Christmastime.

"I need to buy him sooner," Sophie said. "I need to buy him right away! Before somebody else does. What'll I do?"

Allison frowned. "Maybe your mother will lend you the money."

Sophie shook her head. "I already asked her. She says I'm too young to start buying on credit."

"Then maybe she'll give you money for doing extra work. I get paid to take the trash out—when I remember." She looked at her watch. "We have to get going." She started walking toward the corner.

Sophie touched the store window again. "You stay right there," she said to Weldon. "I'll think of something." He seemed to be smiling at her. She could tell he trusted her.

Sophie turned and nearly ran into a man who was walking close to the buildings. "Excuse me," she said, as she dodged around him. She was wondering if her mother would pay her to empty the dishwasher.

"Wasn't that man the filthiest thing you ever

saw?" Allison asked when they had turned the corner.

"What man?"

"The one you almost crashed into."

"I didn't notice," Sophie said.

"He was carrying two great big trash bags. Didn't you notice that?"

"He's probably a garbage collector," Sophie said.

"He looked like a bum!" Allison went through a break in the hedge around the Woodrow Wilson School.

Sophie followed her onto the playground just as the bell rang.

She wasn't thinking of a man with garbage bags. She was thinking of Weldon, the one-of-a-kind hedgehog. She was thinking of him right there in the front of the window where everybody could see him.

2

Sophie was subtracting twenty-eight from thirty-five during math when she had an idea. She would give Mr. Berger at the toy store all the money she had right now. She could tell him she was saving the rest and would have it soon. Then he could put a sign on Weldon that said he was sold already. That way no one else could buy him.

At lunch she told Allison her idea. "I could take the money right after school today. Then Weldon would be mine—sort of."

Allison clapped her hands. "That's a great idea. We can talk to Mr. Berger on the way home."

The rest of the day Sophie could hardly sit still. She was afraid someone would go to the Humpty Dumpty Toy Store that very afternoon and buy Weldon. When she got to the store after school, Weldon would already be gone. It was such a terrible thought it gave her a stomachache.

As soon as school was over, Sophie ran so fast Allison could hardly keep up with her. When she got to the window she let out her breath in a long sigh. Weldon was still there. His eyes glittered at her and he smiled his hedgehog smile. "You're going to be mine," she told him. "Maybe today."

Allison was already opening the door. The bell jingled cheerily, and Sophie followed Allison's red coat inside. The air in the store was filled with the smell of pine. Near the counter was a real Christmas tree, decorated with painted wooden ornaments. An electric train ran around the bottom of the tree. Every so often a white puff came out of the engine's smokestack and the train whistled. Allison stopped at a display of dolls. In the center of the display was a tall bride doll, dressed in a

long, cream-colored satin gown decorated with tiny pearls. She had on a veil edged with lace.

Sophie didn't care about dolls, not even dolls in beautiful wedding gowns. She went over to the window to see Weldon. If she leaned past a purple rhinoceros she could almost reach him.

"Don't touch!" the man behind the counter said in a booming voice.

Sophie jumped back and turned with her hands behind her. But the man was looking at Allison. Allison had her hands behind her, too. Her face was pink.

"Don't touch what you can't buy," the man added.

"But I want to buy her," Allison said. Her face was very pink now. "I mean—I'm planning to buy her. How much is she?"

"Two hundred twenty-nine dollars," the man said. "Shall I wrap her up for you?"

Allison's face almost matched her coat. She shook her head.

Sophie went up to the counter. "Is Mr. Berger here?" she asked.

"He's out sick. What do you want him for?"

Sophie looked at Allison. She was staring hard

at a castle made of plastic blocks, hands still be-hind her back.

"I want to buy that hedgehog in the window," Sophie managed to say.

"Forty-one ninety-nine. Plus tax."

"I don't have that much yet," Sophie said. "I have twenty-one dollars and seventy-eight cents saved up. I want to pay that much today. Then you could put a sign on him to say he was sold. I'll bring the rest when I have it."

"No layaways," the man said. "Not on a special item like that hedgehog." He frowned down at Sophie over the cash register. "How do I know you could get the rest of the money? If you didn't I'd have lost a sale."

"But—" Sophie started.

"No but's. Whoever can pay for him can take him home. Bring me forty-one ninety-nine—plus tax—and he's yours. Till then, he stays where he is."

Sophie felt her eyes start to burn. She blinked very hard. "Thank you," she said. She grabbed the belt of Allison's coat and gave it a tug. The bell jingled again as the two of them scurried out the door.

"What an awful man!" Allison raged when they were outside. "I wouldn't have hurt that stupid bride doll."

Sophie looked through the window at Weldon. He was still smiling, as if he hadn't heard what the man had said. She knew he wouldn't want to go home with anyone else.

"Don't worry. I'll think of something," she told him. But her stomach hurt more than ever. She leaned her forehead against the glass and felt her eyes start to burn again.

"Look!" Allison said. "It's that bum."

Sophie rubbed her eyes and turned to look where Allison was pointing. A man was sitting on the sidewalk in front of Rudowski's Market. He had a dark beard and long, tangled hair that stuck out from under a knitted cap. His jacket was torn and dirty. On the pavement next to him were two fat plastic garbage bags.

In front of him on the sidewalk was a coffee can. A sign with crooked red letters was leaning against the can. I'M HUNGRY, it said. PLEASE HELP.

As they watched, a woman came out of the market with a grocery bag in one hand. She dropped something that clattered into the can as she walked past him. The man was hunched against the wind. He didn't look up.

"Don't get too close," Allison whispered. "He might have a disease or something."

"He's just dirty," Sophie said. But she stayed close to the curb as they walked around him. "When we get to your house we have work to do," Sophie told Allison. "We need to think up a plan to get me twenty dollars. Fast."

Sophie sat in the middle
of Allison's bed with Tiger, Allison's orange cat,
curled in her lap. "How much money do you think
that sidewalk man gets from begging?" Sophie
asked.

Allison shrugged. "A lot, I bet."

"Maybe I could *beg* enough to buy Weldon."

"You're nuts. Your mom would never let you."

Tiger purred as Sophie rubbed behind his ears. "You're right. Read me the whole list," she said.

Allison held up her tablet and read. "One, unload dishwasher." She looked up. "If your mom will pay you to do it." She went back to the list. "Two, bottles and cans. Three, money on sidewalk. Four, coin thing on pay phones. Five, make hotpads and sell."

Tiger dug his claws lightly into Sophie's skirt. Sophie tapped his paws. "I *hate* making hotpads. And last time the only people who bought them were our mothers."

"It was the color. Nobody wanted that puke green. We could get different color loops."

"Loops cost money." Sophie leaned forward to see the list and Tiger jumped to the floor. "Did we only come up with five ideas in all this time?"

Allison nodded. "Unless you count begging. I think five is a lot!"

"It would be if they were any good." Sophie flopped over on the bed. "I'll *never* get enough to buy Weldon," she groaned. "And somebody else will take him home. Probably to give to some spoiled rich kid—like Veronica Martin. What if somebody bought him for Veronica Martin? I couldn't *stand it!*"

Allison stretched and stood up. "I'm starved. Let's go get something to eat."

"Again? Marie gave us brownies and milk when we got here."

"That was ages ago."

Allison opened her door and peeked out. She

looked up the hall and then down the hall. "Coast is clear—no Sam. Let's go."

Sophie followed Allison to the stairs. She was still thinking about money. Even if her mother would pay her to unload the dishwasher, Sophie was pretty sure she wouldn't pay much. Allison said people found money in pay phones all the time. But Sophie never had. Not once. And the only money she'd ever found on the sidewalk was a penny. That left collecting bottles and cans for the five-cent deposit. She'd have to find hundreds of them.

"Where you going?" Allison's three-year-old brother, Sam, was standing at the bottom of the stairs in his denim overalls.

Allison groaned. "We're going to get a snack. And you can't come with us."

"I wanna snack, too," he said.

"You can't have one."

"Can too," Sam said, and stuck out his tongue.

Allison rolled her eyes. "You already had brownies."

"So did you!"

"Yeah, but Marie says you eat too much junk.

Then you won't eat your meals. All you eat is snacks. She says—"

"That's it!" Sophie exclaimed. "That's how I can get money."

Allison looked from Sam to Sophie. "How?"

Sophie grinned. "By not eating lunch! Mom gives me lunch money every day. Instead of buying my lunch, I'll put the money in my bank. She says our school lunch costs nearly ten dollars a week. If I saved that and my allowance, too, I could have enough in two weeks. Just two weeks!"

Allison shook her head. "You can't skip lunch. Mrs. Callahan won't let you."

"I'll say I brought my lunch. She won't even know."

"But Sophie, you'll die of starvation!"

"I'll just eat more after school," Sophie said. "And a big breakfast."

Sam's eyes had gotten very big. "Is Sophie going to die?" he asked.

"No, silly," Allison said. Then she laughed. "She's going to di-et."

4

The next morning, when Sophie and Allison passed Rudowski's Market, the man was sitting on the sidewalk again. He looked exactly the same as before.

"Do you think he's been there since yesterday afternoon?" Sophie asked.

Allison shook her head. "He probably went home last night to count all his money."

"He looks cold," Sophie whispered. His hat was pulled far down over his ears, but his nose and cheeks were red. It made Sophie shiver just to look at him. She pulled her coat closer around her neck. "Very cold."

"He looks dirty," Allison said.

A man came out of the market with a newspaper and a cup of coffee. He dropped a quarter into the coffee can and stepped into the street to hail a cab.

Other people were walking past the man on the sidewalk without looking at him. Sophie wondered how many people put money in his can.

Allison stayed as far away as she could when they walked around him. But Sophie went close

I'M hUNGRy PLEASE HELP

and looked into the can. There were two quarters and a dime in the bottom. The man didn't look up at her. He didn't move.

Sophie hurried past. Maybe begging wasn't such a good way to get money after all. If the man was hungry, that little bit of change wouldn't help him much. He couldn't even buy a hot dog for that.

When they got to the toy store window, Sophie forgot the sidewalk man. Weldon was in the same place, with his nose almost against the glass. But now there was a sprig of holly behind his ear. "Hi, Weldon!" Sophie said. "I hope it's warm enough in there. It's awfully cold out here."

Allison pulled at her coat sleeve. "Let's go. I don't want that guy inside to see us."

"It's a free sidewalk," Sophie said.

But Allison didn't wait.

"You'll be coming home with me in no time," Sophie told Weldon hurriedly. "You just stay there. I have a really great idea to get the money. And Weldon—try to look *ugly*." She hurried after Allison.

At morning recess, Sophie didn't play foursquare with Allison and Heather Hardisty and Sarah Epstein the way she usually did. She leaned against the fence and tried to think of a way to keep Weldon from being bought by somebody else. She'd been thinking and thinking all morning. Mrs. Callahan had scolded her for daydreaming twice. But still she hadn't come up with an idea that would work.

The thing to do was to get him out of sight somehow. If no one could see him, no one would buy him. But with that terrible new man in the store, she wouldn't be able to hide Weldon. If Allison hadn't gotten so close to that bride doll before, the man would have yelled at Sophie just for touching him.

Allison. A glimmer of an idea began to form in Sophie's mind. If Allison would—

"Of course Elizabeth-Rose will be queen!" Veronica Martin's prissy voice interrupted Sophie's thoughts. "She was the ruler of Toyland last year and she'll be the ruler again this year. Nobody in the whole school has a better doll than Elizabeth-Rose. Nobody."

Veronica was standing in the middle of a circle of girls and boys, her hands on her hips.

"I got a brand new Hovercraft for my birthday," Jason Davidson said. "It can stay up in the air without even touching the floor. Maybe every-body will vote for my Hovercraft instead of your stupid doll."

"That's dumb! A machine can't be the ruler of Toyland," Veronica scoffed. "That would wreck the whole pageant."

It was the pageant Mrs. Callahan had been talk-ing about when she'd scolded Sophie the second time. Every year the Woodrow Wilson School put on a pageant at holiday time. It was called *Babes in Toyland,* and everyone had to be in it.

Everyone also had to bring in a favorite toy so the stage would look like Toyland. Every year one toy was elected ruler. The person who owned it got to be its voice and speak the ruler's lines. Last year it had been Veronica's doll, Elizabeth-Rose. She was a beautiful doll. Nearly everybody had voted for her. Even Sophie had.

But after a while, Sophie had wished she could take back her vote. Everyone in the class felt that way. "Her hair is real and her head is made of fine porcelain," Veronica had bragged, over and over. "She's a reproduction of a genuine antique."

Finally, Jason had threatened to drop his battle tank on Elizabeth-Rose's porcelain head. Veronica had boasted about all the lines she got to say as queen clear until spring vacation.

"Elizabeth-Rose will be queen again, just wait and see," Veronica said now. "All the fourth and fifth graders will vote for her. She's a reproduction of—"

"Elizabeth-Rose won't be queen this year," Sophie heard herself saying.

"Oh?" Veronica turned and glared at Sophie. "And who will? Not that ratty old Raggedy Ann you brought last year."

Sophie felt her face get hot. Raggedy Ann was *not* ratty. But she bit her lip to keep from saying it. "I won't be bringing Raggedy Ann this year. And there won't be a queen. It will be a king. *My* king. His name is Weldon. He's a collector's item—one of a kind."

5

"**Y**ou really told Veronica Martin," Allison said at lunchtime. "Nobody'll vote for dumb old Elizabeth-Rose once they see Weldon. It's a good thing you thought of saving all your lunch money. The voting is next week."

Sophie nodded and crunched a bite of the apple Allison had given her. Allison's peanut butter sandwich smelled wonderful from across the table. Sophie patted the lunch money in her pocket and took another bite of the apple, chewing as slowly as she could. She was trying to make it last, but it was already down to a skinny core. It wasn't a very big apple.

"What if somebody else buys Weldon before you've got enough, though?" Allison asked. "That would be awful!"

Sophie nodded again. She wasn't sure what had made her say that about Weldon being king. She just couldn't stand hearing Veronica say one more word about her precious doll. But now she *had* to get Weldon in time for the election. If she didn't, she'd have to bring Raggedy Ann in again. Veronica would make fun of her. It was too awful even to think about.

"I've got an idea," she told Allison. "But you have to help."

"Help? How?"

"Come to the store with me and—"

"You're not going to ask me to go inside again?"

"Just once," Sophie said.

"Never. Not till Mr. Berger comes back."

Sophie's idea wouldn't work without Allison. "Please," she said. "Please! I'll play a game of Hi-Ho! Cherry-O with Sam if you'll help me."

Allison thought for a minute. "Five games," she said.

"*Five?*"

"Five!"

"All right," Sophie said. "Now listen!"

"I can't believe you're making me do this," Allison said after school. They were hurrying toward the toy store, the first snowflakes of the year blowing in their faces.

"It'll be easy," Sophie assured her. "All you have to do is pretend to trip. The boxes will fall over and everyone will look."

"Everyone will look at *me*!" Allison protested. "I'll die!"

"You won't die."

"That awful man will throw me out!"

"I'll be doing the hard part," Sophie said. "You don't want someone else to buy Weldon, do you? You don't want Elizabeth-Rose to be queen of Toyland again!"

Allison shook her head. "Okay. But remember. Five games!"

Inside the toy store, Sophie stood very close to the window and waited. For a long time, nothing happened. Maybe Allison had chickened out. Sophie's stomach growled. Her head felt funny. When she'd stood up in music class after lunch, she'd felt so dizzy she'd almost had to sit down again. Sophie waited, thinking about pizza—and double cheeseburgers.

Then, as she was imagining herself cutting into a huge chocolate layer cake, there was a terrific crash over behind the doll display. She heard the sound of boxes falling. A woman screamed.

"It's all right, folks," Sophie heard the clerk say. "It was only the plastic dinosaurs."

Moving like lightning, Sophie leaned past the purple rhinoceros and snatched Weldon up. She held him for just a moment, snuggling him close, and gave him a kiss on his pointed nose. Then hurriedly, she took the sprig of holly from behind his ear and stuffed him under a giant panda at the back of the window display. She put the holly on the purple rhinoceros and stood back, just as Allison appeared. Allison's face was bright pink again. The clerk was behind her.

". . . be more careful next time," he was saying. "You might have been hurt."

Outside, Allison burst out laughing. "You should have seen his face!" she said. "All the boxes went down, and I fell right in the middle. He checked to see if any stupid dinosaurs were broken before he came to help me. A woman bawled him out for it, too. It was great!"

Sophie stopped at the window. "Look," she said to Allison. Weldon was nowhere to be seen. Sophie tipped her head to the right and leaned way down. She could just make out Weldon's nose and his two bright eyes peeking out from under the giant panda. "Nobody will see him there."

"Good. Now all you have to do is get the rest of the money," Allison said, "in time for the election."

The sidewalk man was still in front of Rudowski's. Snow had made a little ridge around the edge of his knitted hat, Sophie saw. I'M HUNGRY, she read as they hurried past him, staying close to the curb.

So am I, Sophie thought. "Let's go," she said. "I need one of Marie's brownies."

"Me too," Allison agreed and started to run.

"I need *ten* of them," Sophie added, running after her.

6

"Could I unload the dishwasher from now on?" Sophie asked her mother at dinner that night.

Mother smiled. "I'd like that. But you can't reach all the shelves."

"I could use the stool."

"That's a good idea, love. It's sweet of you to help. I'm always so tired after work."

Sophie pushed a piece of macaroni with her fork. Her mother thought she was sweet. How could she ask to be paid for helping now? She'd figured it out—to get Weldon in time for the voting at school, she needed to earn nearly five dollars besides her lunch money. The chore idea wouldn't work. She hoped some of the others would.

She finished her second helping of macaroni and cheese and ate the last bite of salad. Then she finished her second glass of milk. "Is there any dessert?" she asked.

Mother looked at Sophie's clean plate. She looked at the empty serving bowls. "You can have an orange," she said. "You certainly are hungry tonight. Has Allison's housekeeper finally stopped filling you kids up with sweet snacks after school?"

Sophie thought of all the chocolate chip cookies she'd eaten at Allison's house. She couldn't let her mother know she'd skipped lunch. "No, but there weren't enough today. And Sam ate too many." That was true. Sophie would have liked to eat every single one of those cookies, and Sam had had five.

Mother took an orange from the bowl on the buffet. She handed it to Sophie and watched as she peeled it. "Was there a man on the sidewalk by Rudowski's when you came home from school?"

Sophie bit into an orange segment and nodded.

"He was there yesterday, too. And this morning."

"He was there when I went to the market after work. You didn't talk to him or go near him, did you?" Mother asked.

Sophie shook her head. "Just close enough to look in his can."

"I don't want you to go even that close to him." Mother gathered up her dishes and took them to the sink.

"Why not?"

"Because he's dirty and disreputable, and we don't know anything about him."

Sophie spit an orange seed onto her plate. "We know he's hungry. It says so on his sign."

Mother shook her head. "Maybe he is and maybe he isn't."

"I'm pretty sure he is. There wasn't very much money in his can. Not enough for a hot dog."

"He might not use the money he gets for food. He might use it for alcohol. Or drugs."

Sophie thought about that. "Then he'd still be hungry! Allison says he probably earns a lot of money begging. She says maybe he gets more that way than if he had a real job. I don't think she's right, though."

Mother sighed as she gathered up Sophie's dishes. "I don't think she's right, either."

"Did you put any money in his can?"

Mother paused with the dishes in her hands. She looked at Sophie and then away. She shook her head.

"Why not?"

"I don't know, Sophie."

"Because he's dirty and dis—dis—?"

"Disreputable. No, that's not it. I just couldn't decide whether it was right to give him money or wrong."

"Wrong?" Sophie couldn't imagine how it could be wrong to help someone who was hungry.

Mother put the dishes in the sink. "It's complicated. If he really needs help, he should go to one of the places set up to help people like him. Social services or something. It might be better *not* to give him money. I don't want to encourage begging."

"Allison says he probably likes begging. Do you think he likes it?" Sophie asked.

"I don't know. Some people would rather ask for money from other people than earn it themselves. Maybe it's easier than keeping a job."

"It doesn't look easy to me. It looks cold." Sophie took her milk glass to the sink.

Her mother shook her head as she turned on the water. "I just wish the man wouldn't sit by the market. We've never had any homeless people in this neighborhood before. It makes me nervous."

"Homeless? You mean he doesn't have anyplace to go at night?" Sophie couldn't imagine what that would be like.

"He could go to a shelter, I suppose," Mother said. "There must be one. I never thought we needed one around here. Some people won't go to shelters, though."

"What if he didn't? Would he have to sleep right there on the sidewalk?"

Mother rinsed Sophie's glass. "I don't know. Maybe. He might sleep in a doorway. Or an alley. You say there wasn't much money in his can?"

"Two quarters and one dime."

"Maybe if he doesn't get enough to satisfy him here he'll move on. I hope he will. I don't like him to sit where you and Allison walk to school."

"But if he doesn't get enough money, he'll get hungrier and hungrier," Sophie said. She thought about how she'd felt today with only an apple for lunch. "And what if he came *here* from someplace else where he didn't get enough? And someplace else before that? He could starve. Couldn't he? He could starve right to death!"

"I don't think so," Mother said, putting the glass into the dishwasher. "He'd get help first."

"But that's what he's *asking* for," Sophie said. "His sign says, 'Please help.' "

"Oh, love, that's not the kind of help I meant."

7

Sophie lay very still in her bed. She could hear the wind outside her window. It howled. It whistled. Even under her warm pink quilt she shivered at the sound of it.

Most nights before she went to sleep, Sophie thought about Weldon and what it would be like when he came home with her.

He would have his own special place on the radiator by the window. From there he could look out during the day when she was at school. He could watch people going by down on the sidewalk. He could watch pigeons the way Tiger did.

At night she would take him to bed with her. She would put her arm around him, and his little pointed nose would rest against her cheek.

It would be better than having a little brother like Sam. It would be almost as good as having a cat who slept on her bed. And her mother wouldn't be allergic to Weldon.

But tonight she couldn't help thinking about the sidewalk man. Where was he? She wondered if he was lying on the cold cement by the market. She wondered if he had a pillow. Or a blanket.

Sophie looked around her small room. The soft glow from her night-light lit it all. It lit the dresser where Raggedy Ann sat. It lit the shelf with her books and games. It lit the desk where her spelling workbook was and the top of her radiator where Weldon would live.

What would she do with her things if she didn't have a room to keep them in? Would she have to carry them with her all the time? Even to school? If she did that, Roger Logan might steal them. He had stolen her pencil box last year in second grade.

If she carried her things in plastic bags like the ones the sidewalk man carried, she'd never be able to put them down without watching them. Not even to play foursquare at recess. And her clothes. Would she have to carry those with her, too? Her shoes and her boots and her patent leather purse for Sundays?

Sophie snuggled farther under her quilt. She could smell the clean smell of soap on her skin. Where did the sidewalk man take a bath? she wondered. Where did he go to the bathroom? No wonder he was dirty. It wasn't his fault. She would have to tell Allison that.

Sophie yawned and closed her eyes. She pushed the sidewalk man out of her mind and thought about Weldon instead. She smiled. He was safely waiting for her right now under the giant panda. She'd buy him next week, and they'd show Veronica Martin! Everybody in school would vote for Weldon to be king of Toyland. She'd get the five extra dollars she needed somehow. She would start looking for bottles and cans tomorrow.

The wind whistled at her window. Sophie

opened her eyes again. She had seen the sidewalk man in her mind. He was curled up on the hard sidewalk with a garbage bag under his head.

Was he still hungry? The sidewalk man didn't have Marie's cookies and Mother's dinner to make that achey, empty feeling go away.

Even if giving money encouraged begging, she hoped lots of people had put money in his can after she looked this morning. She hoped he'd gotten enough for a whole big submarine sandwich from Rudowski's. And something hot to drink. And dessert. She hoped so.

8

After school the next day, Sophie and Allison stopped in front of the Humpty Dumpty Toy Store. Sophie bent down to look for Weldon. He peeked out at her from under the panda's round tummy. "Another dollar ninety-five today," she told him. But she was too hungry to stay by the window long. She and Allison hurried on. Marie had promised to make butterscotch brownies with walnuts.

The sidewalk man was in front of the market. He looked as cold as ever, hunched over his can. Allison crinkled her nose as they passed him. "I don't care if it's his fault or not," she said into Sophie's ear. "He's so dirty he smells bad."

"It's too windy to smell anything," Sophie said.

"You're so hungry your nose probably isn't working."

Sophie's stomach growled. Allison could be right, she thought. She'd gotten dizzy again when she stood up for the spelling bee that afternoon. And then she'd missed the very first word. It was the first time she'd ever gone out in the first round. She'd been thinking about Marie's butterscotch brownies.

"Later, in Allison's kitchen, Sam started to cry. "Sophie got more brownies than I did!" he said. "It's not fair!"

"Sophie needs her strength," Allison said. "She's going on a bottle and can expedition."

"Me too! I want to go, too!"

Allison took Sam's hand and pulled him away from the table. "Let's go play Hi-Ho! Cherry-O," she said. "Just us two."

Sam grinned. "All *right*! And I'll win. I bet you spill your bucket every time!"

"Thanks," Sophie said as Allison followed Sam up the stairs. She put on her coat and mittens, then took the trash bag Marie had given her and went out. The sky was gray. It would be getting dark soon, Sophie realized. She would have to hurry if she were going to find twenty cans. That would earn her one whole dollar.

Half an hour later, Sophie felt like crying. She had looked in litter cans and along the curbs. She had even gone into the alley behind the stores where the big trash bins were. So far she had found only four cans and one bottle. She had looked in the pay phone in the lobby of her own building. Nothing. And she hadn't found even a penny on the sidewalk.

She was hungry again, too. She passed the cleaners and the flower shop. There were no cans or bottles in the litter can by the curb. The sidewalk man was in his place in front of Rudowski's. Maybe he had already found all the cans in the neighborhood, Sophie thought. He could have gone looking while she was in school. He could look again after she went home. He could look all night.

She glared at him when she went into the market to return her finds. He could get money begging. It wasn't fair for him to take *her* cans!

The market smelled of pickles and fried onions. Sophie's mouth watered. She was so hungry she almost spent the quarter Mr. Rudowski gave her. But she thought about Veronica Martin. "Nobody in the whole school has a better doll than Elizabeth-Rose," she'd said. Sophie put the quarter carefully into her pocket.

―――――――――

When Sophie left the market, she hurried around the sidewalk man. She didn't look at him as she headed for the toy store.

She leaned down to see Weldon. There were his bright black eyes. "I'm trying," she told him. "Honest. Just wait till Saturday. I'll start early. And I'll look for cans all day." She put her hand against the window.

The toy store door opened, its bell jingling, and Sophie stood up hurriedly. A woman in a fur coat came out, carrying a huge box. It looked big enough to hold the bride doll. Sophie stood against the window as the woman went by, her high heels clattering. The woman passed the sidewalk man with barely a glance.

Sophie stamped her foot. "She should have given him some money," she muttered. "Lots of money! She's rich."

The giant panda looked back at Sophie, its eyes blank.

9

Saturday morning Sophie woke up very early. By the time her mother got up, Sophie had already made her bed and dusted her room. She ate a big stack of the pancakes her mother made. Then she asked if she could go looking for cans and bottles.

"You aren't still saving for that hedgehog," her mother said.

Sophie nodded.

"He's awfully expensive. Wouldn't you rather have something else? You could buy that lovely unicorn with the money you already have."

Sophie shook her head. "I want Weldon. With my lunch money, I have nearly enough—" Sophie shut her mouth quickly. But it was too late.

"Sophie! Is that why you've been so hungry all the time? You've been skipping lunch?" Her mother's voice was sharp. "Sophie?"

"Yes. But it's okay—"

"It is *not* okay." Mother folded her arms across her chest. "You need all your meals to grow and stay healthy!"

Sophie explained, then, about Weldon and the pageant and the election and Veronica Martin. When she had finished, her mother sighed.

"All right, love, if it's that important to you, maybe we can compromise. You may save your lunch money until you have enough, but you have to make yourself a lunch to take to school with you every day." She sighed again. "I'll cover the cost of a sandwich and some fruit. But as soon as you've bought Weldon, I want you eating the school's hot lunch again. Understood?"

Sophie nodded. "Understood." She was very relieved. It had been harder than she expected, skipping lunch.

"Now, off you go on your bottle and can expedition. Wear your hat and scarf. Stay right in the neighborhood. Don't talk to strangers. Don't go near that man by Rudowski's. And be careful!"

Sophie grinned. "I will."

Two hours later Sophie was very tired, but she was happy, too. She had found eight cans and two bottles in the laundry room of her own building. And she had found a dusty quarter just under the edge of one of the dryers. Near the cleaners she had found a cardboard carton with six empty beer bottles.

Then she had thought of school. Under the hedges around the playground she had found nine cans. And someone had left a two-liter bottle next to the slide. Now her bag was so heavy it dragged on the sidewalk.

She stopped to tell Weldon on her way to Rudowski's. She could see a lot of people in the toy store. The bell kept jingling as people went in and came out. The gorilla with the leather face was gone, Sophie noticed. So was the unicorn. "Soon," she promised Weldon. "You'll have a home, too. And you'll be a king. King Weldon of Toyland!" He smiled out at her. The panda looked very heavy. She hoped Weldon didn't feel too squashed.

She was just about to leave when Mr. Berger came to the window with a customer. As he picked up a fat, plush pig, he saw Sophie and waved. Sophie waved back, glad to see him. Maybe that other man would go away now that Mr. Berger was back. She hoped he wouldn't notice that Weldon wasn't in his usual place. Mr. Berger liked Weldon almost as much as Sophie did. She hoped he was so busy waiting on customers that he wouldn't have time to even think about Weldon.

It was beginning to snow as Sophie passed the sidewalk man. Her bag clinked and clattered behind her. He must not have been looking for cans this morning, she thought. Good thing for her. He had pulled his cap down farther than ever against the blowing snowflakes. His hands were jammed deep into his pockets.

When Sophie came out of Rudowski's, her money jingling in her pocket, the sidewalk man wasn't in his place. His bags were there, and so were his can and sign. Snow was beginning to stick to the empty sidewalk. A woman hurried by, pushing a bundled-up baby in a stroller.

Sophie looked up toward the toy store. The sidewalk man wasn't there. She turned and looked the other way. There he was—down on his hands and knees, peering into the narrow space between Rudowski's and the flower shop.

Sophie stood and watched to see what he was doing. He reached into the pocket of his jacket and took out a waxed paper package. Carefully, he unwrapped a limp half sandwich.

He took a quick bite. Then he held the rest of the sandwich out toward the dark space. His lips moved. Sophie could hear his voice, very low, but she couldn't tell what he was saying.

She wondered if he could be crazy. Marie said that lots of street people were crazy. They ought to be locked up, she said. The sidewalk man certainly looked crazy, talking to himself like that.

But soon Sophie saw something move. A thin, dirty orange cat stuck its head out from between the buildings. There was a dusting of snow on its head. One ear was ragged and torn. Crouched low to the ground, it moved one paw and then another.

The man, still talking quietly, stayed very still. The cat moved very slowly closer, its ears flat, its whiskers twitching.

Then, with a sudden pounce, the cat snatched the sandwich and melted back into the darkness. The man looked after it. With a nod of his head, he pushed himself up from the pavement and stuffed the waxed paper into his pocket.

Sophie turned toward Rudowski's window. She pretended to be reading the signs as the sidewalk man walked past her, but she was thinking very hard. When he had settled himself behind his sign, she turned and hurried home.

10

Sophie looked at the money piled up on her desk. She had counted it twice. There was a lot now—thirty-two dollars and thirty-eight cents. Using her mother's calculator she had figured it out: only nine more dollars and sixty-one more cents, and she would have enough to buy Weldon. Except for tax. She wasn't sure how much that was. She would have to ask. But with her lunch money and another good day of collecting bottles and cans, she was pretty sure she could do it. She could get Weldon in time to take him to school for the election. She could.

But, looking at all that money, Sophie kept remembering the woman in the fur coat. She had come out of the toy store with that big, big box and walked right past the sidewalk man without even looking at him. That woman had been rich. But she hadn't helped. Not even a little.

Sophie saw in her mind the sidewalk man on his hands and knees. She saw him holding out his sandwich to the cat—the thin, dirty, *disreputable* cat.

Sophie shook her head to make the picture go away. She thought about Veronica Martin and Elizabeth-Rose with the porcelain head. She thought about the voting all the kids would do next Friday. She imagined Weldon wearing a crown and herself saying the lines of the ruler of Toyland. She imagined everyone, even Veronica Martin, clapping at the end of the pageant—for her. For Weldon.

But still she could see the sidewalk man. She could see the cat.

Sophie sighed and began counting her money again. She put a quarter on one side of her desk and a quarter on the other side. She put a dollar on one side and a dollar on the other side.

"I was afraid of that," she said later that afternoon, as she and Allison reached the window of the Humpty Dumpty Toy Store. There was Weldon, right in the front of the window again. The prickles on the top of his head looked the tiniest bit crumpled, but his plaid bow was as crisp as ever. "I was afraid Mr. Berger would find him."

It was snowing hard now. The store's bell jingled as a man, holding the hand of a little boy in a blue snowsuit, opened the door. They stomped the snow off their feet as they went in.

"We have to hurry," Sophie said.

"Okay," Allison said, "but I'm warning you, if the other man is here, I'm coming right back out again."

The other man was nowhere to be seen. Mr. Berger was waiting on a customer. The girls stood by the Christmas tree and waited. When he was finished, Sophie asked him her question.

He smiled a big, friendly smile. "A layaway? I might consider a layaway. Of course you know, that's a very special animal you're talking about. He's a collector's item—"

"One of a kind," Sophie finished. "I know. I've been saving all my allowances and all my lunch money. But I was afraid somebody would buy him before I had enough."

Mr. Berger nodded gravely. "That's possible. Especially at this time of year. Especially . . . " He looked toward the window and rubbed his chin. Then he peered down at Sophie. After a moment, he winked. "Especially now that he's come out from under that panda bear."

Sophie's cheeks began to feel hot.

"So tell me, how much money did you bring for the first installment?" Mr. Berger asked.

Sophie patted her black patent leather Sunday purse. "Sixteen dollars and nineteen cents."

"But, Sophie!" Allison raised her eyebrows in surprise. "You said you had—"

"Sixteen dollars and nineteen cents," Sophie repeated firmly. "And I can bring money in every week until he's paid for. I'm collecting bottles and cans to turn in at Rudowski's."

"But *Sophie!*" Allison said when they left the store, Sophie clutching her official layaway receipt.

"There's no way you'll have him in time for the pageant. Elizabeth-Rose will be queen again. What happened to the rest of your money?"

Sophie held up her purse. "It's right here."

"Then why didn't you give it to Mr. Berger? Veronica Martin will drive us all crazy!"

"I know." Sophie had been thinking and thinking about that. She'd been thinking about what Veronica would say when she had to bring Raggedy Ann again. She shrugged and started walking, scuffing the snow with her boots as she went.

In front of Rudowski's the sidewalk man sat, hunched over his coffee can. There was snow on his cap and his shoulders and his beard. There was snow on his two garbage bags. Sophie stopped.

"Now what?" Allison said.

Sophie didn't answer. She opened her purse. She took out an envelope. On the outside she had printed carefully, FOR THE SIDEWALK MAN. She walked over to the coffee can.

"Sophie!" Allison said behind her. "You're not supposed to go near . . . "

Sophie leaned down and put the envelope in the can. "There's sixteen dollars and nineteen cents in there," she said, her voice trembling a little. She said it loud enough for Allison to hear, and she didn't look at the man.

The sidewalk man said nothing. He didn't look up. Snow fell on the envelope inside the coffee can.

Sophie backed away. "Let's go," she said to Allison, and began to run.

"I don't get it," Allison said when she caught up. "That man didn't even say thank you. He's dirty. Maybe he's crazy. Why did you give him half of your money?"

Sophie whirled around on the sidewalk. All of a sudden, she felt very good. "Because he's hungry."

11

By the next Saturday, most of the snow had been shoveled or plowed away. Only ridges of it were left along the curbs. Sophie and Allison went looking for bottles and cans. Allison found seven and Sophie found four. Together they found two more. They went to Rudowski's to turn them in.

"Hey, look!" said Allison. "The sidewalk man is gone!"

Sophie stood still, looking at the place where the man had been. It was strange to see the sidewalk empty. It was almost as if a tree had disappeared, or a building. A woman carrying a shopping bag walked right across the place where the sidewalk man's sign and coffee can had been.

After a moment, Sophie took the money from her left pocket and put it with the money in her right pocket. It made an impressive bulge. She would be able to give all ten dollars to Mr. Berger now instead of only five. "Where do you suppose he went?" she asked.

Allison shrugged. "Maybe the police chased him away. Marie says they could do that."

Maybe he went to find a neighborhood where people would give him more money, Sophie thought. Or maybe he went to a shelter. She hoped, wherever he was, he was warm.

With her half of the money Mr. Rudowski gave them for the cans and bottles, Sophie bought a doughnut and split it with Allison.

"Sam's coming to the Christmas pageant this year," Allison said, brushing crumbs from her coat. "He won't like Queen Elizabeth-Rose."

"No," Sophie agreed. "He'd like Jason's Hovercraft better."

"It was funny that Veronica didn't even ask about Weldon," Allison said.

"She was just glad Elizabeth-Rose didn't have any competition after all."

"And she only mentioned her fine porcelain head one time." Allison looked at her watch. "I've got to get home. You want to come over for lunch? Dad's making hot dogs. You could have two. Or even three."

"No thanks," Sophie said. "I've got to go make a payment on Weldon."

"Okay. Come over this afternoon, though."

As Sophie walked to the Humpty Dumpty Toy Store, she thought about the sidewalk man. She wished she knew where he had gone. It wasn't fair, she thought. It wasn't fair not to know.

Then she thought about the cat. She remembered how it had snatched the sandwich and disappeared. The sidewalk man had only smiled and nodded and gone back to his place. She smiled now, too.

At the window, Sophie paused to look in at Weldon. His black nose was pressed against the glass, almost as if he'd been waiting for her. Pinned to his plaid bow was a small, hand-lettered tag that said SOLD.

She touched the cold glass next to his nose. "Don't mind about Veronica and Elizabeth-Rose," she told him. "You can be king of Toyland next year."

Mr. Berger saw her through the window and waved. Sophie patted the money in her pocket and went inside.